Pilchard
and the Big Surprise

Illustrations by Dyna~~

EGMONT

D0256310

EGMONT

We bring stories to life

First published in Great Britain 2009 by Egmont UK Limited
The Yellow Building, 1 Nicholas Road, London W11 4AN

Endpapers and introductory illustrations by Craig Cameron.

HiT entertainment

ISBN 978 1 4052 4343 8

45938/4

Printed in Italy

FSC
www.fsc.org
MIX
Paper from
responsible sources
FSC® C018306

Egmont is passionate about helping to preserve the world's remaining ancient forests.
We only use paper from legal and sustainable forest sources.

This book is made from paper certified by the Forest Stewardship Council® (FSC®),
an organisation dedicated to promoting responsible management of forest resources.
For more information on the FSC, please visit www.fsc.org. To learn more about
Egmont's sustainable paper policy, please visit www.egmont.co.uk/ethical

Pilchard keeps disappearing and Roley doesn't know why. So Roley goes in search of the runaway cat . . . and gets a big surprise!

One morning, Bob gathered his team together in the yard. He had somebody with him, somebody new!

"Team, I want you to meet Rupert Reekie," said Bob cheerfully.

"Hello, Rupert!" chorused Scoop, Muck, Dizzy and Lofty.

"Mr Reekie's a glass artist," said Wendy. "He makes things by recycling old glass!"

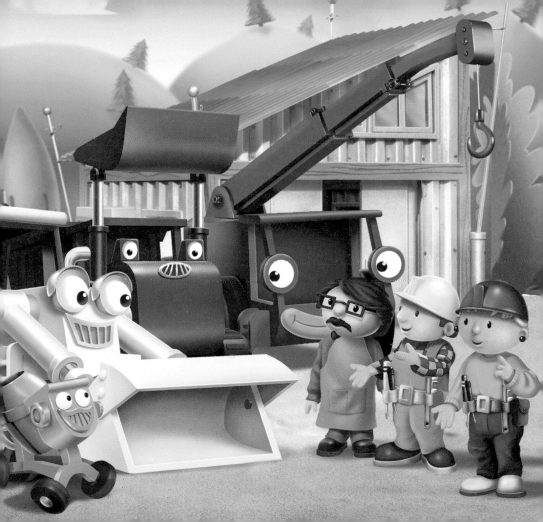

"Rupert and I designed a glass studio together," Bob told the team, "and now we're going to build it!"

Suddenly, Roley rushed into the yard, looking worried. "Pilchard! Where are you?" he called.

"That's Roley," Wendy told Rupert, "and Pilchard is Bob's cat!"

"I've got a cat called Sprat," said Rupert. "He's always disappearing. Cats do that!"

Roley was worried about Pilchard. He couldn't find her anywhere.

"Pilchard! Pilchard!" Roley called. Then, by accident, he bumped into a pile of tyres.

Suddenly, out of the pile crept Pilchard! "Miaowww," she mewed grumpily. Then, with a cross look at Roley, she ran away.

"I'm so clumsy," sighed Roley, sadly. "No wonder Pilchard doesn't want to play with me!"

Roley followed Pilchard to the playground, and raced around after her. Then he slowed down. "I need to be more careful!" he thought. "Being clumsy's what upset her last time."

Even though he was trying to be careful, Roley crashed into the slide. Down slipped Pilchard, landing in a pile of leaves!

"Miaow!" she mewed crossly at Roley and walked off, leaving Roley feeling sad.

Meanwhile, Bob was working on the roof for Rupert's studio when Packer arrived with a big oven on his trailer.

"My furnace!" said Rupert. "Fantastic!"

Packer had something else for Rupert, too – three sacks full of jars and bottles.

"I'll use this hot furnace to melt all the old glass to make new glass," Rupert told the team. "I'm making some stained-glass windows for the roof of my studio!"

Roley followed Pilchard to Scarecrow Cottage, calling after her, but Pilchard dashed off again. Spud came out to see what all the noise was about.

"Pilchard's stopped being my friend 'cos I'm too clumsy," said Roley sadly.

Spud had a brilliant idea. "Why don't you pretend to be a cat? Cats are never clumsy!" He started to walk on his hands and knees and purr, just like a cat.

Roley wiggled a pretend tail. "Pilchard! Come and play with Roley the big, green cat!" he sang. Then he wiggled so hard that he knocked over the hay bales!

Pilchard leapt out from under the hay and miaowed crossly at Roley. Then she ran towards the studio, with Roley chasing after her.

Roley didn't see the sacks on the ground that Rupert was coming to collect . . .

Suddenly, there was a CRUNCH! Roley looked under his roller, and saw lots of pieces of broken glass!

"Oh, no!" he gasped. "I must have run over some of Mr Reekie's glass art!"

Just then, Bob and Rupert arrived with a beautiful stained-glass panel to put in the studio roof. Rupert's cat, Sprat, came to take a look, and tangled himself between Bob's ankles, purring loudly.

"Sprat, no!" cried Rupert, but it was too late. Bob tripped over Sprat, and the glass panel fell to the ground with a SMASH!

"Oh, no!" groaned Rupert. "I spent ages making that panel!"

Roley rolled slowly forwards. "I'm really sorry, Mr Reekie, but I had a bit of an accident with some of your art, too," he said, blushing.

Nervously, Roley showed Rupert the pile of glass he had crushed.

But instead of being angry, Rupert smiled.

"Don't worry, Roley, that wasn't my art! I can melt this broken glass and use it to repair the panel!" he said.

So Rupert sorted the glass into different colours and melted it in the furnace.

Once it had cooled, he moulded it into new shapes.

After some time, the new panel was finished. Bob and the team stood back to admire the new stained-glass studio roof.

"Look, Roley, it's you!" Bob laughed, pointing at the picture, which showed a smiling Roley with Pilchard and Sprat.

"Thanks, Mr Reekie, that's great!" Roley said, beaming. "I wish I knew where Pilchard was, though."

"And where's Sprat?" wondered Rupert.

Suddenly, Roley heard a "Miaowwww!" and saw Pilchard's tail waving from behind a bush. "There she is!" he gasped.

"And look!" whispered Wendy. Huddled around Pilchard were three fluffy kittens. "Pilchard's a mummy!"

Along came Sprat, and rubbed up against Roley. "Sprat must be the daddy," laughed Wendy. "He wants you to be Uncle Roley!"

"Rock and roll!" sang Roley proudly.

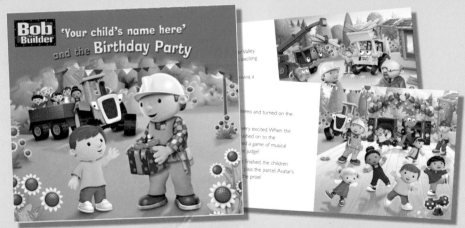